INDIA

Hawaii

Howland island

NEW GUINEA

Lae

PACIFIC
OCEAN

Tahiti

NEW ZEALAND

SCOTLAND

CULMORE

DONEGAL
DERRY
ANTRIM
TYRONE
Ulster
FERMANAGH
ARMAGH
DOWN
MONAGHAN
SLIGO
LEITRIM
CAVAN
MAYO
ROSCOMMON
LONGFORD
LOUTH
Connacht
WESTMEATH
MEATH
GALWAY
OFFALY
KILDARE
DUBLIN
Leinster
LAOIS
WICKLOW
CLARE
TIPPERARY
CARLOW
LIMERICK
KILKENNY
WEXFORD
Munster
WATERFORD
KERRY
CORK

ENGLAND

WALES
PWLL

SOUTHAMPTON

FRANCE

PARIS

Amelia Earhart

Adventurer and Aviator

Written by Ann Carroll
and illustrated by Derry Dillon

Published 2020
Poolbeg Press Ltd

123 Grange Hill, Baldoyle
Dublin 13, Ireland

Text © Poolbeg Press Ltd 2020

A catalogue record for this book is available from the British Library.

ISBN 978 1 78199 842 7

Cover design and illustrations by Derry Dillon
Printed by GPS Colour Graphics Ltd

This book belongs to

To TUIREN Love Etain

Happy 10th Birthday

Amelia's Last Flight (1937)

Beginnings

This story begins in 1895, in the town of Atchison, Kansas, in the United States, with the marriage of Amy Otis and Edwin Earhart.

The bride's father, Alfred, was against the match. Alfred was President of the local Savings Bank and a former state judge. As a person of importance he felt entitled to a better son-in-law.

"The fellow always introduces himself as Samuel Edwin Stanton Earhart," he sighed. "Trying to impress! I cannot think much of him. He is a useless lawyer and earns little. I also hear he is a drinker who cannot hold his liquor so I fear he is a ne'er-do-well!"

Nevertheless the marriage went ahead and the birth of Amelia (called Millie) in 1897 was followed two years later by that of Grace Muriel (nicknamed Pidge).

Millie and Pidge lived for more than a decade with their grandparents – their mother's parents – in Atchison, while their parents settled in Kansas City, where Edwin hoped to make his fortune.

Before leaving, their mother told Grandma Otis, "I don't want you to rear Millie and Pidge as ladies. Don't let them be nice little girls!"

Grandma followed her wishes and perhaps as a result, the children had happy times in Atchison.

Childhood

The girls loved their grandparents' house. It was built on a small hill by the banks of the great Missouri river. All day the river traffic passed – steamboats and fishing boats, cargo vessels and wide flat barges.

From the veranda Millie and Pidge would wave to the boatmen, delighted when they waved back.

Often Millie would tell a story about one of the characters they'd seen on a passing boat, making up his life, deciding his destiny, giving the spur to her own sense of adventure.

Where Millie led, Pidge followed and so did the other children in the neighbourhood.

They went on expeditions along the river banks, climbing trees, making hideouts, trapping rabbits.

An uncle taught Millie to shoot and one day, armed with a rifle, she led a rat-hunting expedition and brought home the day's catch.

Grandma was snoozing in the rocking chair on the veranda.

"Look, Grandma! I shot half a dozen rats!" Millie dumped all six out of a sack at her grandmother's feet.

"Oh, my blessed and merciful God!" Grandma screeched, jumping up from her sleep.

She needed a double brandy to recover.

Then she told her granddaughters, "You are not allowed throw dead rats at your grandma! I blame your uncle with his shooting lessons and will give him an earful. Find another pursuit!"

Deprived of rat-hunting, it was Millie who came up with a new idea.

"Uncle, will you build me a ramp from the roof of the high shed?"

"Why?" Her uncle was cautious after the rat episode.

"See, I'd put this crate at the top, sit into it and slide all the way down to the ground."

Her uncle hesitated.

"It'd be like the roller coaster at the fair in St Louis," Millie continued.

"A roller coaster?" her uncle said, aghast.

"Only it'd be much smaller," she added hastily. "And you'd be helping us find another pursuit like Grandma said and anyway she never comes near the shed so she won't know a thing about it and you're just brilliant at building things! Brilliant!"

She was very persuasive.

"I'll do my best!" her uncle said.

When the ramp was finished Millie climbed the high ladder and clambered across the shed roof to where her uncle held the wooden crate in place. She settled into it.

On the ground, Pidge watched, fascinated. She had no wish to try the slide but thought her sister very brave.

"*It's awful high!*" she called.

"*So much the better!*" Millie shouted and turned to her uncle. "On the count of three push the crate – one … two … THREEEEE!"

The crate rocketed down the first few feet, came off the ramp, flew through the air and landed on the grass below.

Pidge shrieked and their uncle roared. He climbed down as fast as possible, still roaring. He and Pidge rushed to the crate.

"That was mighty glorious!" Millie picked her way out of the wreckage, dress torn, shoes lost, lip bleeding and arms scratched. "That was the best! It was like flying, Pidge – just like flying!"

Moving On

Things didn't go well in Kansas City for Millie's father, Edwin. His career was failing, mostly because of his drink problem.

Then in 1907 his luck changed.

"I've been offered a job in Iowa, Amy," he told his wife, "working for the railroad in Des Moines. It's better pay, enough to buy a house. Once we're settled the kids could come and live with us. What do you say?"

His wife was silent.

"I'll give up liquor, Amy. We'll be a proper family. Won't that be mighty?"

"I guess so," Amy said. "If there's no drinking."

"I promise!" Edwin said.

Everything went well and two years later Millie and Pidge joined their parents.

In Atchison they'd had a home tutor. In Des Moines they went to school.

Millie wasn't impressed. School had too many people, hardly any free time and a teacher who gave orders.

Pidge saw things differently. "But I like all the people in my class," she said. "And the lessons – and I like my teacher too."

"Yes – well, you're not right in the head!" Milly muttered.

But Milly loved reading and wrote well and when her teacher praised her essays and gave her books to read, she began to settle in.

A Change in Fortune

1912 was a sad year for the girls. Their grandparents got ill and died within a few months of each other. The deaths marked the end of their Atchison years.

Still, the family was comfortably off in Des Moines, had a nice house and could afford two servants.

But then Edwin got into money difficulties and the job went wrong and he found alcohol gave him some comfort.

Over the next couple of years his drinking got worse. First the maids left, then the family had to move to a rented house.

One day in 1914 Edwin lost his job.

"You can leave, or I can sack you," the boss said, so Edwin left.

Millie thought: I wish we could go home to Atchison. I wish Grandma and Grandpa were alive. They'd love having me and Pidge.

But there was no going back and the family home in Atchison was sold. The girls were heartbroken.

"It was the end of my childhood," Millie said later.

Edwin managed to stop drinking and found work with the Great Northern Railway in St Paul's, Minnesota, and the family moved again.

Within a year he heard of another better position in Springfield, Missouri, and applied.

"The guy's retiring," he told his wife. "It'll mean promotion and more money if I'm successful!"

He got the job and resigned from his own.

Then the man changed his mind about retirement and Edwin was left with nothing.

He turned again to alcohol.

"Well, Edwin," his long-suffering wife said, "wherever you go next we're not going with you. I'm taking the girls to friends in Chicago."

"You're running out on me?"

"I am, Edwin, I surely am. Now that Ma's will is sorted, I can give the girls a good life. You've noticed I'm sure that the money is tied up in a trust fund so you can't touch it. And just as well!"

In Chicago the girls called themselves Amelia and Muriel, setting aside their childhood.

They went to Hyde Park High School. It was Amelia's last year at second level.

And it's obvious from the yearbook comment that the other students saw her as mysterious:

Amelia Earhart – the girl in brown who walks alone.

What Next?

After school the sisters took different paths.

Amelia enrolled in a Junior College in Pennsylvania but didn't stay long.

"I can't settle," she said. "I want to be doing, not studying!"

Muriel got into Smith College, Massachusetts, and later into Radcliffe (now part of Harvard). She became a teacher, married and had two children, and spent most of her life in Medford, Massachusetts.

In 1917 Amelia went to Toronto in Canada. There she heard about the crowded hospitals, full of wounded soldiers from World War I.

"Well, I guess now that I'm twenty I should be doing something useful."

She trained as a nurse's aide. The young men, some of them even younger than her, had suffered horrific wounds.

The hours in the hospital were long and hard and Amelia got Spanish Flu in 1918. This epidemic killed millions throughout the world, mostly young adults, many of them soldiers.

In the last months of WWI no leaders wanted the enemy to know how badly their armies were affected by this deadly flu and such reports weren't allowed. But journalists could write about Spain which wasn't in the war, so everyone believed that Spain had suffered most from the epidemic and that it must have started there and so it became known as 'Spanish Flu'.

Amelia spent two months in hospital because she was so sick.

"Now you're recovering, would you like to come to an air show," a friend asked, "or would it be too much excitement?"

"Of course I'll come. Standing on the sidelines can't be too exciting! And it has to be better than lying in bed!"

They stood at the edge of the airfield as the small planes soared and dipped and looped overhead.

Suddenly one pilot separated from the rest and headed directly towards them.

Amelia didn't move but her friend shrieked and jumped back.

The plane came closer and closer, then swerved up – up and away!

The friend was very disgruntled. "Well, I surely would like to know what you do find exciting, Amelia. My heart is still jumping!"

Amelia smiled and afterwards said, "I didn't understand it at the time but I'm sure that little red plane said something to me as it swished by."

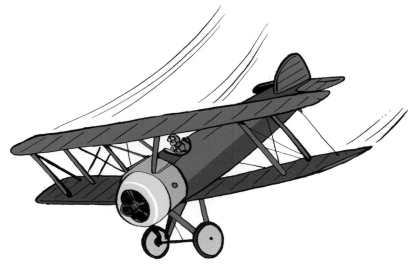

However, it wasn't till two years later that she took a flight for the first time.

It happened on a visit to her parents, who were back together and had settled in Long Beach, California. To entertain Amelia, her father paid a pilot to take her on a flight.

The experience delighted her.

"I knew then I had to fly," she said.

She had her first lesson on January 3rd 1921.

And afterwards she said, "Now I know what I want to do in life!"

Nothing was going to stop her becoming a pilot.

She saved a thousand dollars for flying lessons and walked 6 miles every time along the coast to the airfield to take them.

"I mean to look the part too!" she said.

She cropped her hair and slept in her brand-new pilot's jacket until the leather looked worn enough to have flown thousands of miles.

She bought a plane and called it *The Canary*. By May 1923 she had her Pilot's Licence.

Life seemed perfect.

But her parents didn't stay together. Her father was drinking again and in the following year after twenty-nine years of marriage they finally divorced. (Edwin died in 1930, aged fifty-eight.)

Then her grandmother's trust fund ran out and there was no money for the upkeep of *The Canary*, which had to be sold.

To keep herself, Amelia took a job as a social worker in Medford, Massachusetts, where her sister now lived.

She was back in the drudgery of everyday life.

It must have seemed like the end of the dream to make flying her career, but in fact the dream was only beginning.

Flying High

Amelia stayed connected to flying.

She joined the American Aeronautical Society and wrote about flying for a number of papers.

In 1927 Charles Lindbergh was the first to fly solo across the Atlantic and he was everybody's hero.

I'd love to be the first woman to fly across the Atlantic! Amelia thought.

And one day she got a phone call asking her to an interview for just such a trip.

"Well, Miss Earhart – Amelia – I reckon you're by far the best woman for this flight," George Putnam told her.

George was a publicist and publisher and was on the interview board.

"I like your spirit of adventure," he said. "You're not shy either. You talk well and you write well. We can make something of this flying business. Now I'm no pilot, but I'm good at publicity and I intend to make you a public figure, Amelia. You've got style!"

She was the third member of the crew, along with the

pilot and co-pilot, Wilmer Stultz and Louis Gordon.

I'm only keeping the log, she thought, but I'm the first woman on a transatlantic flight!

On June 17th 1928, their plane, *The Friendship*, left Newfoundland off the east coast of Canada and landed after twenty hours and forty minutes in South Wales at Pwll, where there is a commemorative plaque today.

Two days later they flew on to Southampton, on the south coast of England, to a huge welcome.

"The others did all the work," Amelia told everyone. "But maybe one day I'll get to pilot such a flight."

On their return to the States the three were given a ticker-tape parade along the Canyon of Heroes in Manhattan, New York. Later President Calvin Coolidge received them at the White House.

Because she was the first woman to make such a journey, the public wanted to know everything about Amelia.

And George Putnam made sure she was constantly in the news.

Fame and Fortune had arrived.

Queen of the Air

That August Amelia flew solo across North America and back – the first woman to do so.

With George's help she achieved much: she did a lecture tour of the States to packed houses; she became Associate Editor of *Cosmopolitan* magazine; hailed in the press as Queen of the Air, Amelia was a byword for smart, daring and modern and she branded clothing, sportswear and luggage.

She also promoted Lucky Strike cigarettes.

"Maybe Lucky Strike wasn't such a good idea!" Amelia told George one day.

"Well, for Heaven's sake, why not?"

"I just opened this letter from *McCall's* Magazines. They don't want to do business with me. It seems smoking isn't the image they want to project."

"But it's the modern thing for women, honey. It looks smart and does no one any harm!"

Of course no one knew then cigarettes could be a killer. *McCall's* just thought smoking wasn't one bit ladylike.

With George's encouragement Amelia wrote a book about her first transatlantic flight, *20 Hrs. 40 Min.: Our Flight in the Friendship*, which became a bestseller.

George was divorced from his first wife and had two adult sons who liked Amelia, so one day he said, "We spend a lot of time together, don't we?"

"We do," agreed Amelia who was reading the paper and only half listening.

"And we get on well, don't we?"

"We do," agreed Amelia.

"And we have the same interests, don't we?"

"We do."

"And we like each other an awful lot, don't we?"

"Course we do."

"And we both like robbing banks every day, don't we?"

"Oh, we do, we do."

George let the silence gather until Amelia looked up, saw his amusement and grew flustered.

"Sorry, George! No, no … of course we don't like robbing banks! Well, maybe we would if we gave it a go! What are you on about anyway?"

"I'm asking you to marry me!"

"You are? Why are we discussing bank robberies then?"

"Look! Forget banks! Forget crime! Are you going to marry me?"

"Charming! Yes, yes. OK. Though I don't like changing my name."

In 1931 they were married and, as it happened, no one called Amelia by her married name. She was so famous it was George who became known as Mister Earhart.

The Powder Puff Derby

One of my favourite phobias is that girls, especially those whose tastes aren't routine, often don't get a fair break. **Amelia Earhart**

Amelia reckoned that women pilots didn't get the same chances as men.

For one thing, she thought, it's not fair that air races are for men only!

So Amelia promoted the first women's Air Derby in August 1929. This was a nine-day race from Santa Monica, California, to Cleveland, Ohio.

Twenty female pilots entered the competition.

Will Rogers (a famous actor and comedian of the time) immediately called it the Powder Puff Derby and the name stuck.

The fluffy title seized the imagination of the press and public. Everyone knew about it which suited Amelia just fine.

It was a tough competition and bad things happened. Marvel Crosson died when her plane crashed. Blanche Noyes had to put out a fire on her plane before continuing. Pancho Barnes crashed into a car that drove onto the runway as she was landing and her plane was wrecked.

There were many other incidents, yet the Derby was seen as a success, and a crowd of 18,000 came out in Cleveland to cheer the pilots and especially the winner, Louise Thaden. Amelia came 3rd.

But the men-only competitions didn't change.

So the women continued separately and made sure the media noted that their times and speeds were very close to those of the men.

Then in 1936, one well-known competition, the Bendix Race, at last allowed women pilots to compete with men.

And what happened?

In 1st and 2nd place were Louise Thaden and Laura Ingalls, while Amelia came 5th.

After that no one could argue that men were better aviators than women.

The Ninety-Nines

In November 1929, Amelia was one of the founding members of The Ninety-Nines, an organisation for women pilots.

"Why the name?" someone asked her.

"Because 99 women pilots turned up to our first meeting," she said.

She was its first president, from 1931 to 1933.

Her aim was to support women pilots through scholarships, training, competitions and advice.

The Ninety-Nines later bought her childhood home in Atchison, Kansas.

Now it's a museum and looks just as it did when she was small.

Today the organisation has over 5,000 members and every year a scholarship in Amelia's name is awarded to a woman pilot.

Amelia Earhart
Birthplace Museum
Amelia Earhart was born July 24, 1897
In the home of her grandparents,
Alfred G. and Amelia Harres Otis.
The home was constructed circa 1860.
The Birthplace Museum is owned by
The Ninety-Nines, Inc. International
Organization of Women Pilots

Something about Amelia

Amelia received many awards. Among them:

The Cross of the Knight of the Legion of Honour from the French government.

The Gold Medal from the National Geographic Society (presented by President Hoover).

The Distinguished Flying Cross from Congress.

In 1932 she at last flew solo across the Atlantic.

"I intend to land in Paris," she said, and no doubt thousands of Parisians were looking forward to her arrival.

However, strong winds took her off course and she landed in the north of Ireland, in a field at Culmore, in Derry – a tiny place.

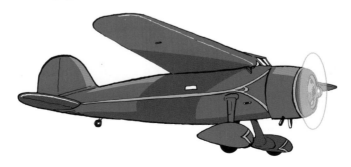

There was no crowd, just a startled farmer, unused to planes landing beside him.

As Amelia stepped out of the cockpit, he said, "Good day to you, ma'am. Have you come far?"

"I've come from America," she said.

There's no record of the man's response. Perhaps he was speechless, but there is a plaque at the site commemorating the occasion.

During the first half of the 30s Amelia set seven women's records for speed and distance and everyone must have thought, Well, she's done it all really! What else is left?

But there was something about Amelia that made her seek out the next new record.

And it was a challenge no one had tried before.

The Last Big Adventure

I can only say I do it because I want to. Adventure is worthwhile in itself. **Amelia Earhart on flying**

Amelia planned a round-the-world trip. The flight path would follow the equator and be 29,000 miles (46,670 km) long.

She had a plane specially built and called it *Electra*, after one of the brightest stars in the heavens.

After some setbacks she and her one-man crew, Fred Noonan (an experienced aviator), set off from Miami on the 1st June 1937.

They flew from west to east: to South America, to Africa and on to India, arriving in Lae, New Guinea, on the 29th June. Three days later, they were ready to take off again across the Pacific Ocean to California, 7,000 miles (11,000 km) away on the west coast of America.

"Our first stop is a small remote island – Howland Island," she told reporters. "It's 2,556 miles (4113 km) away from here."

"Isn't the journey too far? Even with the refuelling stops there must be a danger of running out of gas?"

"No danger," she said. "The *Electra* has extra-large tanks and we'll also carry extra fuel. And the naval ship *Itasca* will be waiting at Howland to guide us in with radio contact."

They set off at midnight. Amelia had once written about a night flight: '*The stars seemed near enough to touch and never before have I seen so many. I always believed the lure of flying was the lure of beauty and I was sure of it that night.*' So she must have loved her flight across the Pacific.

They neared the Howland Island area. The colossal journey around the world was nearly done – just over 2,500 miles (4000 km) were left.

As the plane came closer, *Itasca* was ready with radio assistance. The surface for landing was flat and nothing should go wrong.

Except it did.

The crew on *Itasca* could hear Amelia but neither she nor Fred could hear them – and the plane was miles off course, though Amelia didn't know it.

At 7.42 am, Amelia radioed: *"We must be on you, but cannot see you – gas is running low. Have been unable to reach you by radio. We are flying at 1,000 feet."*

From barrels of oil the ship's crew billowed smoke into the air, hoping it would guide her towards the island.

Again they heard Amelia, *"We are running on line north and south,"* meaning she was sure they were in the right position to land. But they weren't even near enough to see the smoke.

Then came silence and the ship's crew heard no more.

Electra, the bright star, had vanished.

Afterwards

Afterwards the Air Force, the Navy and the Coast Guard combed a vast area of ocean and searched islands and small outcrops of land.

Not a trace of plane or crew was ever found.

Afterwards, when they stopped looking, Amelia's husband George financed his own search, without success.

Later came the rumours: Amelia was alive and living on some remote island – or, Amelia was held captive by the Japanese.

But no one ever discovered exactly what had happened.

Afterwards Amelia's mother went to live in Medford with her other daughter, Muriel, and died there at the age of ninety-two. She never gave up hope of Amelia's return.

Muriel was a teacher, wrote two books about Amelia, and lived till she was ninety-nine – more than fifty years longer than her sister.

Afterwards George married twice more and died at the age of sixty-two in 1950.

Amelia though lives on, honoured in museums and books and films, remembered always by women pilots everywhere.

Who else has ever been so fearless and adventurous?

The End

GLOSSARY (alphabetical order)

achieve: to reach an aim

associate editor: an editor who is second in importance to the main editor

aviation: flying

aviator: pilot

barge: a long flat-bottomed boat used to carry things on rivers and canals

byword: a person or thing closely connected with a particular quality

canyon: a long, narrow valley with very steep sides, often with a river along the bottom

cautious: careful, avoiding risks

cockpit: the place where the pilot sits in a small plane

colossal: huge

comb: to search very carefully

commemorative plaque: a plate of metal, ceramic, stone, or wood, usually attached to a wall, with words or an image in memory of a person or event

Congress: in the United States, the part of the government dealing with the law

decade: 10 years

destiny: what life will bring to each person OR a force that some people believe controls the future

drudgery: very hard boring work

enrol: to put your name down in order to join a course or a school or group

editor: a person who corrects or makes changes to a book being written by someone, or to a film being made OR a person in charge of a newspaper or magazine

epidemic: an illness that spreads rapidly to many people

exceptional: greater or better than usual

expedition: a journey made by a group of people for a special purpose, especially that of exploration

impress: to cause someone to admire you or something you have done

liquor: strong alcoholic drink

ne'er-do-well: a lazy and useless person who never does anything well

outcrop: a large rock or group of rocks that sticks out of the ground

powder puff: a round piece of soft material used for putting powder on the face or body

publicist: someone whose job is to provide information about a person, product, or an organization

pursuit: following or chasing something OR an interest or hobby

ramp: a slope made with wood or metal or other material that joins two levels (like a wheelchair ramp)

remote: far away and isolated (on its own)

resign: to give up a job by telling your boss you are leaving

scholarship: money given by a school or university to pay for the studies of someone who can't afford to pay

seize: to grab something suddenly and keep it

steamboat: a boat driven by steam, especially a paddle-wheel boat used on rivers in the 19th century

ticker-tape parade: a parade in honour of a someone important or who has done something remarkable, where confetti and streamers etc are thrown from buildings along the way

tutor: a teacher who teaches a child outside school hours OR teaches a small group of students at a college or university

vast: huge

veranda: a long porch with a roof over it, along the front or back of a house

vessel: a boat OR a container such as a cup or bowl used to hold liquids

yearbook: a book in a school or university that has photographs of students and details of school activities in the previous year

Some Things to Talk About

1. Do you think Millie and Pidge had a happy childhood?
2. Amelia was an exceptional person. What were her best qualities, do you think?
3. Did she enjoy taking risks?
4. Do you think boys and girls these days have equal chances in life?
5. Aeroplanes were a marvellous invention. What might be a great invention in the future that would change our lives?
6. Imagine a different end to Amelia's story – one where she survived. What happened next, do you think?
7. Amelia's great dream was to be a pilot. What's your dream?

Timeline

1895: Marriage of Amelia's parents, Amy Otis and Edwin Earhart
1897: Birth of Amelia (Millie)
1899: Birth of Muriel (Pidge)
1897–1909: Childhood in Atchison with their mother's parents
1909: Millie and Pidge move to Des Moines to live with their parents
1912: Death of grandparents
1914–1918: World War I
1914: Edwin loses his job
   The family move to Springfield, Missouri
1915: Millie and Pidge move to Chicago with their mother – the girls call themselves
   Amelia and Muriel.
   It is Amelia's last year at school.
1917: After a stint at college, Amelia moves to Toronto and becomes a nurse's aide to
   soldiers wounded in World War I
1918: Amelia is ill for 2 months with Spanish flu
1920: Amelia visits her parents (who are back together) in California and takes her
   first flight
1923: Gets her Pilot's Licence
1927: Charles Lindbergh becomes the first to fly solo across the Atlantic
1929: Amelia becomes the first woman to fly transatlantic (as part of the crew)
1929: Her parents finally separate and divorce
   Promotes the first women's Air Derby: the Powder Puff Derby
   Helps found the Ninety-Nines, an organisation for women pilots
1930: Death of Amelia's father, Edwin
1931: Amelia marries George Putnam
1931–1933: Is first president of the Ninety-Nines
1930–1936: Sets seven women's records for speed and distance
1932: Flies solo across the Atlantic, landing in Ireland.
1936: The Bendix Race is the first to allow women to compete with men. 1st, 2nd
   and 5th place go to women pilots!
1937: Amelia's last flight